SHADOW SNATCHER

To Elizabeth Hawkins - a great teacher! LK

First published 2012 by A & C Black,
an imprint of Bloomsbury Publishing Plc
50 Bedford Square, London WC1B 3DP

www.acblack.com
www.bloomsbury.com

ISBN 978-1-4081-5485-4

This book is produced using paper that is made from wood
grown in managed, sustainable forests. It is natural, renewable
and recyclable. The logging and manufacturing processes conform
to the environmental regulations of the country of origin.

Printed by CPI Group (UK), Croydon, CR0 4YY

1 3 5 7 9 10 8 6 4 2

recommended by

www.catchup.org

Catch Up is a not-for-profit charity
which aims to address the problem of
underachievement that has its roots in
literacy and numeracy difficulties.

SHADOW SNATCHER

LOU KUENZLER

A & C Black • London

Contents

Chapter 1

Uncle Tony

It was Halloween when Death came to my house.

He didn't wait until it was dark at night. He came early in the morning.

Me and my little sister, Eva, were still eating our cereal.

"Who's that?" said Eva, when the doorbell rang.

"I don't know, do I!" I said.

Eva is only five. I'm thirteen.

The doorbell rang again.

"Maybe it's Max Sounds," said Eva. "I bet he's come to make me a star! I'll be just like Minnie Pink..."

Eva loves Max Sounds. He's from that kids TV show, *The MaX Factor!* Max comes round to an ordinary house. He asks everyone in the family to sing. The winner gets to go to the Grand Final. Minnie Pink is the girl who won last year.

"Come on, Aidan," Eva cried. "Let's go and see!"

"Just eat up," I told her. "It's not Max Sounds!"

The doorbell rang again.

"ALL RIGHT! I'M COMING!" I shouted.

"I bet it is him," Eva gasped.

"It's just Uncle Tony," I said.

It was half term. Mum and Dad were at work. I was babysitting Eva till Uncle Tony came round.

I ran into the hall. I didn't look out of the spy hole. I just flung the door open.

The man at the door was dressed in black from head to toe. He had a long cloak like a monk. The hood was pulled down over his face.

The only part of his body I could see was a bright white hand. It poked out from under the cloak. The hand didn't seem to have any skin on it. Just bone.

"That's a great glove, Uncle Tony," I said. "You must be pretty hot in that costume."

The figure took a step forward.

"Come on in," I said.

That was my first big mistake. Never invite Death in to your home.

Chapter 2

Danger of Death

The figure followed me into the house. He still didn't speak.

"You'd better take your hood down," I said. "Eva will be scared if she sees you looking like that."

The door swung closed behind him, by itself. The whole room went freezing cold. That's when I knew it wasn't Uncle Tony.

"You have to go," I said. "I don't know who you are."

The figure leaned over me.

He was much taller than Uncle Tony. Who was he? Why didn't he say something?

I took a step back, trying to block the hallway behind me. But the silent stranger kept coming. He was heading for the kitchen.

"Stop!" I held up my hand to push him back.

My fingers hit the hard, cold bone of his shoulder. My hand had gone right through his cloak. It was as if there was nothing there. No cloth. No flesh. It felt as if the cloak was made from mist.

I wanted to call out to Eva. I wanted to tell her to run. But I was scared that she would come into the hall to ask why. She always asks questions before she does what she is told.

"My dad is in the front room," I lied. "I'll call him if you don't go!"

The figure spoke at last. "Go on then." His voice was so low, I could hardly hear it. "But he won't come, will he?"

I could feel him looking at me from under his hood.

"There's nobody else here," he whispered. "You and your sister are all alone!"

I couldn't move. It was as if my feet were frozen to the spot.

"Who are you?" I gasped.

The figure took another step forward.

"I am Death," he said. "I have come to take Eva."

Chapter 3

Shadow Snatcher

"Eva is mine!" said Death.

"She is not yours!" I cried. "She belongs here. With us. You leave her alone!"

But deep down, I knew why he had come.

"When Eva was a baby, she was meant to die," said Death.

That was true. When Eva was born, she was very sick. We all thought she would die. I was kept home from school. Dad didn't go to work. We sat in the hospital, waiting.

"But Eva didn't die," I said. "She got better."

After three weeks, the doctors told us there was nothing wrong with her any more.

But there was something wrong.

I noticed it in the park one day. Eva was playing in the sun.

"Look!" I said to Mum. "Eva doesn't have a shadow!"

"Don't be silly!" Mum said. "Everyone has a shadow. It's just the way the sun is shining."

But whatever way we moved, it made no difference. Mum and I saw our own shadows on the ground. But Eva didn't make a shadow.

The doctors did tests, but they couldn't find anything wrong.

Nobody knew why she didn't have a shadow. They told us it wasn't important.

But it *was* important. And now Death had come to collect the little girl who got away.

"I kept Eva's shadow when I let the rest of her go," said Death.

He ran his bony fingers down his cloak. The mist moved. Like shadows.

At that moment, Eva came into the hall.

"Was it Max Sounds at the door?" she called. "Does he want to..."

Eva didn't finish her sentence. Her eyes grew wide. She stared up at Death in his long black cloak. Then she smiled.

"Uncle Tony!" she said. "Is that you?"

There was a flash of light. Death's hand shot out from his shadowy cloak.

"No!" I screamed. "It's not Uncle Tony, Eva. Run!"

Chapter 4

Hide and Seek

Eva ran up the stairs.

"Not that way!" I yelled. "We've got to escape."

But it was too late. Eva was already at the top of the stairs. I had to follow her.

We hid behind her toy basket. I could hear Death coming up the stairs after us. I thought about jumping out the window. But Eva's room is too high up.

"I'm coming! Ready or not," called Death.

For him this was just a horrible game!

"I'm going to throw something at him," I said to Eva.

I looked in the toy basket, but it was full
of soft toys. I found a bright pink plastic box.

"My Max Sounds Singing Machine,"
cried Eva. "You can't throw that!" Her big
brown eyes were full of tears. She grabbed
the toy and wouldn't let go.

Instead, I picked up a doll from the floor.

"No! Not Baby Polly!" yelled Eva.

Death was right outside.

"When he comes in," I said, "I am going to throw the doll at him. You have to run, Eva. Run downstairs. Get help. Understand?"

Eva nodded her head. She was too scared to speak.

The door swung open.

"Hide and seek?" said Death. "I'll count to ten."

He turned away from us. His hooded head was hidden in his hands. He really was counting.

"One..." he said.

"Two..."

Eva grabbed me tightly. Her fingers dug into my skin.

"Three... Four..."

I let go of Eva's hand.

"Five..."

"Go!" I hissed.

With one hand I pushed Eva towards the open door. With the other hand I threw the doll. I aimed right at Death's head.

WHAM!

A bolt of light shot across the room.

Eva hadn't taken a step. She was still right beside me.

"Baby Polly!" screamed Eva.

The doll lay on the floor.

Her plastic head was on one side of the room. Her body was on the other.

Death laughed.

"That could have been Eva," I thought. "She could have been torn in half as easily as a doll."

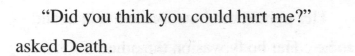

"Did you think you could hurt me?" asked Death.

"Maybe I can't hurt you," I said. "But I bet I can beat you!"

"Really?" Death sounded interested.

I was thinking fast.

I thought about how Death had laughed as he came up the stairs. This was all just a game to him. Maybe Death was a bit like Uncle Tony after all. Uncle Tony can never say no to a bet or a dare.

"Yes!" I said to Death again. "I bet I can beat you in a game!"

"I will take the bet," said Death. "If you win, Eva will live a long life. But if I win, she will die today."

Eva sobbed.

"She hasn't even got a shadow," said Death. "She has nothing to protect herself from me."

Chapter 5

The Contest

Death looked down at the pink plastic
microphone in my hand.

It belonged to Eva's Max Sounds
Singing Machine.

"I bet I can beat you at singing," I said.

"Singing?" Death hissed. "You want me to sing?"

"Yes!" I nodded. "That's the game. You have to win a singing contest."

"But," growled Death. "I can't..."

"Can't what?" I asked. "What can't you do?"

Death's voice was quieter than ever. "I can't sing!" he hissed.

"Too bad!" I handed him the microphone and looked through the list of songs on the Max Sounds Singing Machine.

41

At last, I found the perfect song. Minnie Pink! Eva's favourite.

I looked at the screen on the machine. This is where the scores flash up. Eva has made me play this game with her a million times. She always wins.

"It's easy," I told Death. "You sing the song and the machine judges you. If it shows hearts, it means you're good. Skulls mean you are bad."

I closed the curtains and turned off all the lights. For a moment it was horribly dark.

"Ready?" I said. "You start."

Eva held up a torch. A pool of yellow light fell on Death. His huge, black cloak made strange shadows on the wall.

Death started to sing. His voice sounded like two cats fighting.

"You've got to believe. Really believe," sang Death.

A row of three skulls showed on the
screen.

"Oh dear!" I said to Death. "That's a
terrible score."

Now it was Eva's turn.

I took the torch from her. She was so scared, her legs were shaking. "Don't worry," I said.

I put the torch up on the bookshelf. A ring of light shone around Eva. She didn't make a shadow.

Death laughed.

"Stay in the light, Eva," I said. "Stay in the light and sing the best that you can!"

Chapter 6

Playing Fair

Eva started to sing.

The moment the music started to play she wasn't scared any more. When she reached the chorus, she was smiling.

Three hearts sparkled on the screen. Top score!

ZAP!

A ball of light shot out of Death's sleeve. Eva ducked just in time.

"You're not playing fair!" I cried.

"Fair?" said Death. "The bet was that *you* could beat me. But it was Eva who sang, not you. You haven't beaten me!"

"Not yet," I said. But I knew exactly what to do. Death had come to take Eva because she had no shadow... But what if I could lend her mine?

Death raised his arm. He was about to throw another ball of light.

This time I was ready.

"Don't move, Eva!" I cried, and I jumped forward, so I stood between Eva and the torch. My shadow fell across Eva just as Death threw his deadly ball of light.

ZAP!

SMACK!

The ball of white light hit my shadow. It was as if it had hit a wall of bricks.

It bounced back and hit Death right in his chest, exploding like a firework.

Death fell back. His cloak seemed to tear into a million pieces.

Black shadows shot out in every direction.

His cloak was not made of mist. It was made of shadows!

Shadows Death had stolen.

One sleeve of his cloak rose up into the air. It floated towards Eva.

"Help!" yelled Eva.

"Stand still!" I shouted. "It's your shadow. It's coming back to you."

The shadow touched her. It took the shape of a little girl.

"My shadow!" cried Eva. She waved madly. Behind her on the wall, the shape of her shadow waved back.

"Very clever!" said Death.

"You told me Eva hadn't got a shadow. You said she had nothing to protect herself from you. Now she is safe!" I laughed.

"You have won!" said Death. "For now."

He vanished.

Eva threw herself into my arms.

"We did it!" I cheered. "We beat Death, Eva. You and me."

"We beat him with the help of my Max Sounds Singing Machine," smiled Eva.

Attack of
the Killer Frogs

Lily saw the giant frogs in the garden. Mum
and Dad don't believe her. But Lily knows
the frogs are coming to get her. Soon. Maybe
even tonight… Can Lily escape the attack
of the killer frogs?

ISBN 978-1-4081-5268-3
RRP £5.99

Big Shot

Danny's having a hard time at school.
His best mate Ash told everyone about
his ballroom dancing, and now he's been
banned from the sports trials. How can
Ash and Danny prove their skills on the
playing field now?

ISBN 978-1-4081-7409-8
RRP £5.99

Rainbow Boots

All the cool kids have Rainbow Boots. All except Denzil. So he tells a lie about the special pair he's going to get… Soon the lies are piling up. Can Denzil find a way out of his web of lies?

ISBN 978-1-4081-7408-1
RRP £5.99

Looking for a longer read?

**WIRED UP
CONNECT**

Sports

Horror

Real Life

Science Fiction

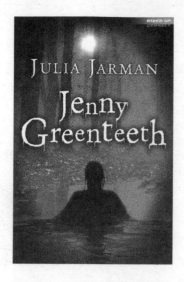